DIRECTION

A Journey Out of Fear and Guilt

TEMILOLUWA ASAGUNLA O.

DEDICATION
I dedicate this book to the Almighty God. He counted me worthy and gave me the privilege to pen down this priceless piece. Unto him, I return all the glory.
I also dedicate this book to everyone who has battled against guilt and fear all their lives.
I am grateful for your lives and God's love for you.
God wants to use this book to enlighten you on freedom. Therefore, read and be free.

CONTENTS

FOREWORD

The collective message of 'DIRECTION' is one that turns the spotlight away from portraying Christianity as a religion, rather than Christianity as a lifestyle, whilst paying commendable attention to the foundations. It is a well acclaimed, untrue notion that the entirety of a Christian revolves around attending church programmes, fasting, and praying. In order to fully live the lifestyle of the Kingdom, it is truly imperative that Christians possess the requisite knowledge. In a world where the supernatural controls the physical, it is unacceptable and unexpected of a Christian to live life without the consciousness of our responsibility embedded in Revelation 5:10: "And hast made us unto our God Kings and Priests: and we shall reign on the earth."

In the most pleasing manner; storytelling, this book exposes the basics and fundamentals of Christian living in ensuring a sustainable relationship with Abba – a relationship with the understanding of it. Particularly, the hands through which the penning of this book is made possible is one to always anticipate following the passion that fuels it. The prowess of the author in presenting seemingly complex principles into easy and fascinating, through intriguing steps and processes, is one that perpetually keeps me in awe. Her desire and interest in transforming lives is one that makes this book a must-read. Dear reader, in pursuit of the necessary knowledge in Hosea 4:6, this is what this book reveals.

-Adetomiwa Fowowe

INTRODUCTION

When you get inspiration about certain things, God wants to use you for, you can only imagine how strange they sound at first!
How does God expect me to write a book before this year runs out? How would it be possible? Like how?
I was inspired to write this book in the most unexpected place and time. All I ever wanted at that moment was to surrender to God because I bore the weight of so much for so long.
Imagine finishing a book in less than two days! It was the situation of this book in the end, mind-blowing!
Without mincing words, I can assure you that this isn't any random written piece. It is a record of confirmed facts from the Holy Spirit, carefully and intentionally conveyed using a narrative approach.
A story of a man having a conversation with his beloved son. "Undoubtedly, unveiling this to the world will lead many to redemption from fear and guilt", I said to myself.
Fear limits you, and guilt kills you! They are both destructive mechanisms of the devil to disturb our minds and make us neglect salvation. I have been a victim for so long and coming out of it opened lots of doors for me. It marked the beginning of a new fresh start for me and I am sure it will for you too.
On second thought, I am deeply humbled by the privilege given to me by God to write this short but priceless treasure. It helps to reveal our true identity and the authority we control as Christ's followers. It is a great thing to start your journey with Christ by first reading this book as it takes you on a smooth imaginative

ride!
Therefore, beloved, I will admonish you to enjoy the ride and be open-minded to learn!

CHAPTER 1

A JOURNEY TO THE OLD

As he took his seat to begin eating, a flash of his old ways captured his mind. Josh was a youngster with big dreams. He lived his life like he was to figure out everything himself; with his setbacks drowning him like a hopeless stray dog. His old life could be characterised as one without direction, identity, and purpose but with massive daydreams of unrealistic and self-made success. Although Josh always attended church services with his parents, he still felt bound to a set of laws that wasn't revealing Christ to him. He struggled with failure, heartaches, uncertainty, fear, troubles, and unrest. Life and religion tossed him around for so long. "Thank God for grace, grace changes everything," he said as he began to eat. Josh immediately stood up to leave the restaurant as it was getting dark. As he drove home, he played his favorite song: **'*YOUR WINGS BY LAUREN DIAGLE.*'** He fell in love with this song the very first time he accidentally came across it on YouTube. It reminds him of how God shows up for his people at every moment, giving them rest through it all. While listening and nodding his head continuously, vibing to the reggae rhythms the music gave, he suddenly remembered his planned conversation with his son, Adam, that evening. "Welcome honey, welcome Dad!" Everyone came running excitedly to welcome Josh back from work. "Muah! Muah! Thank you, baby." Josh said after giving Anne a soft kiss on her lips. "Dad." Adam called, "remember you promised me a conversation tonight. I want to know how and why you believe in Jesus so much." "Well, son, get ready! It is about to be a long and interesting night," Josh said as he laughed in a goofy manner and playfully lifted Adam upon his shoulders with him to his room. After a relaxing shower, Josh got out of the bathroom to kick-start a life-changing conversation with his son. He still had his face towel wrapped around his neck when he began searching his wardrobe for his nightwear. Adam on the other hand, sat quietly on the bed, watching his dad put on his nightwear and at the same time, curiously anticipating the long-awaited conversation with his dad.

"Adam, you believe God is good right?" Josh asked. "Well dad," Adam began, rolling his eyes, "I hear that often, but I desire to know why you and mum refer to God as good. I deeply want to know God and Jesus too." Josh smiled and began, "God is the all-supreme God. He is the one and only true God. Jesus Christ is His son, and you must have heard sayings of how He came into the world to save mankind from sin. He was sent by God to reconcile us back to God since we fell short of God's glory." "Hmm, this is interesting," Adam stated and opened his eyes in awe. "Tell me more, Dad," he added. "I am glad you have gotten interested and I would love to share my personal salvation story with you.

CHAPTER 2
THE ENCOUNTER

"I grew up attending church regularly but never really understood salvation," Josh stated as he paused to drink from the glass of water he kept on the dressing table. "I mean, I have heard several teachings and sermons, but it still felt like I was missing something crucial. I struggled for years, trying to keep up with the laws of Moses being preached to me–laws about how I am supposed to dress; what I am to watch or listen to when I wanted to freely do what I wanted to do; how not to lie; how not to steal and so on. Truth is; I still found myself doing a lot of things because nobody really explained things to me; all they did was turned me against things my flesh wanted to do that I couldn't leave on my own."

He continued, "fast forward to my first year in high school, I was still caught up in the space of struggling with what to do and what not to do. I could remember skipping classes to smoke in the bush with my friends. It felt normal and I lacked the Holy Spirit who is to help me understand why certain things aren't meant for me as a child of God; who is to help me unlearn and subdue the flesh rather than me doing it on my own. I lacked Christ, and every teaching I had received at that time was centered on doing things right on my own, rather than through Christ. Christianity was portrayed as strict. You must do everything right; which made it even harder. I continued to be as confused, and as guilty as a trapped rat. I was stuck and burdened, hoping that I would be free from the mental torture and the fear of going to hell soon. One Friday night, I had an encounter. I never really knew true salvation could set one free from instilled fear and condemnation until that night." Eagerly, Adam interrupted him and asked, "can you tell me about the encounter, Dad?" "It was in camp, a church camp meeting," Josh responded.

He added, "every summer, the church my parents and I attended always organised annual camp meetings for teenagers. They see it as a time to inculcate good Christian habits into young people and possibly teach them about some doctrines with a little time of fun to end camping. This particular camp that I was to attend was one accompanied by a mix of emotions for me. A part of me wanted to open up myself to Christ, while the other wanted to attend camp to just chill with the cool church guys, and you know, keep life moving like we always do in every camp."

At this point, Adam kept paying attention and adjusted himself to get extra comfortable. Josh continued, "my friends and I were rebels, we usually ended camp meetings gaining nothing. This time was totally different – I desired newness." With a bit of surprise, Adam asked, "Dad, isn't living life and being cool fun? "I know it sounds fun, but there is more to life than chilling at the most confusing state of one's life. After my encounter, I noticed accountability, attentiveness, and responsibility in me. I felt empowered to do things right with Christ, leading my every move. People started to place value in me as the sudden change in my life was evident everywhere I found myself."

Delving right into narrating the incident, Josh said, "on that beautiful night, we were taught about the Holy Spirit. Prior to camp, Minister Bernice, our lead youth pastor, always showed keen interest in me as I was one of those who led choruses during worship and praise sessions in the teen's church. I guess it is a gift that came naturally from God and has stayed with me even till now. God doesn't take His gifts from you; how you use them is what matters. I only wanted to serve in any capacity I could. "At least my works would please God," I always said.

I believed in God but didn't know how to grow into intimacy with him. I still struggled with control of my mind. I felt submission to Christ was hard and demanding.

As Christians, we must understand that the initial plan of God for us was to commune with our spirit, and his will and purpose for us align immediately with his. But since we fell, our spirits became weak and the flesh took over. In salvation, there's a place of believing in Jesus to get saved but also a stage of the activation of the Holy Spirit to kick-start the spirit-to-spirit conversation on how things should be done as a spirit being saved by God and for God.

Salvation clearly defines the fact that we are a spirit who possesses a soul and live in a body and so the body shouldn't control us but the spirit of God with which we fellowship with.

After the teaching, an altar call was made for those who wanted to re-dedicate their life to Christ wholly and, as I recited the words after the pastor, I immediately felt at ease but still desired to be filled with the Holy Spirit. The teaching had first stirred me up to strongly believe in Christ and now I wanted his spirit to fill me up. I suddenly stepped out, made my way to the altar, and began to acknowledge the presence of God's spirit in my life. I desired an intimate relationship with his person as I was told the Holy Spirit is a person. I kept asking him to fill me up as I am weak and needed him in my life."

CHAPTER 3
THE INFILLING OF THE SPIRIT

"I kept praying, pouring my heart out sincerely and unashamedly. I wanted the Holy Spirit and nothing more. I was determined to empty myself of every guilt and fear I felt.

I was sure my friends and other teenagers who knew how unserious I was, saw a Josh determined to change that very moment and as I focused and kept praying. I felt someone's hand on my shoulders, whispering to me, "Don't be afraid Josh, let him speak through you. You have received him". It was so calm and peaceful and immediately I keyed into those words, I felt overwhelmed and began to loudly speak in other tongues. Speaking in other tongues is one of the many gifts and evidence of the spirit of God and manifesting this gift got me so excited." Josh narrated.

Josh paused and said, "After that day, a couple of my curious friends asked what really happened to me the day before and how I really felt. I told them, it is not something I could explain and, as I was about to ask if they knew who tapped my shoulder, they immediately told me how Minister Bernice came to encourage me while I was praying and how she jumped for joy when I switched to tongues. Till now, I remain very grateful for her help and the intentionality she showed towards me. She showered me with real love and helped me to understand Christian living myself, through the scriptures. She didn't force me to do anything, she would always call to encourage and put me through, as I studied the word of God. She told me to be very conscious of the Holy Spirit and never leave him out of each of my decisions or situations.

The whole encounter with the Holy Spirit was an unforgettable experience. I wasn't in control of myself and it felt like something greater overruled every burden and pain I felt from inside and it was evident. It marked the beginning of a turnaround in my life, and I felt fresh strength and hope. The Holy Spirit now dwelt and still dwells in me."

He further narrated, "I started a journey of genuine intimacy with God after my encounter. It was like I had finally found a trusted friend to call in my every trouble and distress. God has goodies in stock for everyone, and he fulfills every promise at the time he's sure it is best for us. He sent his Holy Spirit to help us live and communicate with him consciously as the spirit he created us to be. He freed us from the control of our bodies and empowered us to learn how to exercise divine authority as joint heirs with Christ. I trust God so much and I am undoubtedly sure he will always give me the best. After the encounter, I also began trusting every process. I got revelations about my identity and mission gradually and the Holy Spirit began to work through me to achieve everything that was revealed. I am grateful for every decision I took, every lessons learnt including every mistakes made. It was all to shape me into what God wanted for me."

Noticing how interested Adam was, Josh added, "speaking to you, I now understand why God was so particular about me even when I was far but desired Him. He single-handedly and intentionally brought me close because he saw desire and willingness. From consistently studying God's word, I figured he loves everyone the same way and he is ready to reconcile any willing and confused heart back to himself as long as they desire him". "Wow dad", Adam exclaimed, "your story is brief, but indeed special."

"Adam, go grab your Bible," Josh instructed. Adam hurriedly

rushed to his room, grabbed his Bible, and came back to Josh panting and stretching forth his Bible to his Dad. "Here it is, Dad," he stated while trying to catch his breath.

> *Therefore, if anyone is in Christ, he is a new creation; the old has gone, and the new has come!*
>
> *-   (2 Corinthians 5:17)*

"Dearest son," Josh said whilst looking at the Bible, "this passage wholesomely gives a summary of the transformation I encountered the moment I believed in Jesus Christ. Unlike the old times, when I was made to believe salvation doesn't come easy and that I have to be holy all by myself, while strictly following the Laws. There is a new life now and Jesus Christ came to earth, fulfilled every Law of Moses on our behalf, and died on the cross to place us above the Law. We now have abundant life, peace, and freedom only through Christ. Christ gave me a new life and identity. Looking back, I do not want to imagine the fear and guilt that enslaved me because I didn't know the salvation truth. Even the Bible in psalms 103 reveals that God forgives all our sins as long as we believe and fear him. He doesn't chastise us harshly nor condemn us because His love and compassion for us are great and he does understand that, we who desire him may fail sometimes but he's ready to take us through a full fulfillment journey.

"He will not constantly accuse us, nor remain angry forever. He does not punish us for all our sins; he does not deal harshly with us, as we deserve. For his unfailing love toward those who fear him is as great as the height of the heavens above the earth

- (Psalms103:9-11NLT)

I also figured that trying to save yourself by good morals and deeds is Self-righteousness and it will always fail." He further stated, "it is even unbelief because you are believing in yourself to save you and not Christ. Let me tell you another fact; through the death of Christ, faith, hope, love, and grace were released unto mankind, to help us understand and appreciate salvation." "Dad, can we go to bed now?" Adam interrupted his father. "I really want to take this conversation slowly. I also wish to ponder on the scripture we just read before going to sleep," he added. "Okay Adam, run along now." Josh said tapping his son's back repeatedly," we would discuss it during breakfast tomorrow." Adam landed on his bed with his thoughts flying around. Now, he understood why his parents believed so much in Jesus Christ. "Salvation is priceless," he said softly and then grabbed his Bible to read the passage his father read earlier again. *If any man be in Christ, he is a new creation.* "This is deep! I will await further conversations with dad tomorrow," he said as he drifted into sleep.

CHAPTER 4

FURTHER CONVERSATIONS

"Morning my munchkin", Anne woke Adam up with a kiss and quickly added, "it is time for devotion." Adam, knowing how important devotion was, got up, washed his face, grabbed his Bible, and hurriedly ran after his mum. It was a Saturday morning and devotion started with Josh leading the choruses as usual. After much dancing and praising, Anne handled the day's topic from the church's instructional manual. "Breakfast is ready boys," Anne called as she served the food on the dining table. "It's potato and fried egg!" Adam shouted excitedly with a big grin on his face as he joyfully approached the table. Josh, who was already seated, was trying to conclude his personal bible study. He was on it before Anne called for them.

"Welcome my boy; I hope you are excited about today's conversation." "Yes, Dad! I have been anticipating another interesting session with you since I woke up," Adam answered Josh. Anne quickly interrupted after observing the boys for a while, "You boys are successfully making me jealous. I can't wait to have my own baby girl soon." She said jokingly, she then turned to leave the boys for the kitchen. "Dad," Adam began, "you made mention of four things yesterday; hope, faith, love, and grace. Can you please take me through them?" he asked. "You are such a smart kid," Josh said, "I wasn't expecting you to remember so much. I plan to touch the three most important of them in our conversation today, so don't worry, you will know all you need to know". "Okay, Dad," Adam nodded in excitement and smiled.

"I am sure you had time to reflect on our long talk yesterday," Josh asked. "Yes, I did reflect. I even slept off while on it," Adam answered. Josh smiled and said, "that is expected. Meditating on Christian conversations brings peace and so, you dozing off isn't new to me. Today, I would first like to talk to you about the fall of man and our restoration." "I …. I think I know a little Dad," Adam quickly stated, interrupting his father. "Well, go on," Josh said, ready to listen. Adam then answered, "I read in Genesis that God created man to worship him and take dominion here on earth but unfortunately, we were deceived by the devil and disobeyed God's instructions. This took us far away from God. He was totally displeased but regardless, his love for us prevailed despite how much we hurt him."

"Exactly son, what else do you know?" Josh further probed. Adam answered, "I also recall that God used people like Noah, Abraham, David, Joseph, and so on to fulfill His will at every moment. He called Abraham the father of Faith because he believed so much in God, even without knowing all about God. Abraham learnt about God as he walked obediently with God and I'm still in awe of the kind of Faith he had. God also gave instructions apart from the law given to Moses on how his people can be saved from their sins temporarily like killing a ram and so on. There are lots of accounts and past events encompassing man's fall and our journey to restoration by Jesus Christ carefully structured by God."

"Wow, Adam! I am more than impressed. It seems to me that I only have little to talk about then. From all you have said, I have now concluded that you have been paying absolute attention to teaching both here at home, during devotion, and in church. I guess I am as interested as you and mum in knowing and serving God truthfully," Adam said smiling. He added, "well, that is beautiful, son. I will also advise you to read the scriptures as you are led by the spirit. It is as important as eating food to stay healthy every day because it helps you get personal knowledge and understanding about God who you believe in, and his methodologies. It is good for Christians to know God for themselves to sieve things preached to us these days through God's spirit. As your father, I am obligated to help you understand truthful Christianity basics, and as time goes on, your maturity in faith will depend on you and what you feed on. By feeding, I mean sermons you listen to. A lot of misconceptions, false teachings, and beliefs fly around these days with pastors getting distracted and preaching laws and unnecessities, rather than Christ himself. You see the law only came to reveal us as sinners. It came to help us understand how disconnected we are from God. It is evident in the book of Romans 3: 21.

Adam quickly got up to read the scripture with his dad as Josh opened the Bible. "Oh my"! Adam opened his mouth in surprise. "That's not all, son," Josh said, "God used the law to temporarily keep us in order till Jesus finally came to execute the salvation plan. Christ's death and resurrection brought a permanent solution to sin. Paul said in his letter to the Romans:

> *"For we know that the law is spiritual, but I am of the flesh, sold under sin. For I do not understand my own actions. For I do not do what I want, but I doth everything I hate .Now if I do what I do not want, I agree with the law, that it is good. So now it is no longer I who do it, but sin that dwells within me. For I know that nothing good dwells in me, that is, in my flesh. For I have the desire to do what is right, but not the ability to carry it out. For I do not do the good I want, but the evil I do not want is what I keep on doing. So I find it to be a law that when I want to do right, evil lies close at hand. For I delight in the law of God, in my inner being, but I see in my members another law waging war against the law of my mind and making me captive to the law of sin that dwells in my members. Wretched man that I am! Who will deliver me from this*

body of death? Thanks be to God through Jesus Christ our Lord! So then, I myself serve the law of God with my mind, but with my flesh, I serve the law of sin."

-        (Romans 7:14-19,21-25)

This scripture implies that, even though our flesh still fails sometimes, we are no longer called sinners and the spirit is constantly working in us to subdue the flesh. Our identity has now been changed in that we are now sons of God alongside Jesus Christ. Now, this brings me to the three main terms I will love to talk about today; Grace, Faith, and Love," Josh ended and began the topic of the day.

CHAPTER 5

FAITH AND GRACE

Josh adjusted his posture and began, "unlike Mercy being a legal term, Grace is described in the Bible by Paul as an undeserved privilege. You see for Mercy, the offender is just pardoned. It doesn't mean he or she won't always be known as an offender. Grace surprisingly wipes out every allegation! It is a mystery that wiped out all condemnation and sinful history. In Grace, we now have a new master, Jesus Christ, who has taken us away from the country of sin into the dispensation of freedom and responsibility. Imagine changing a lost and forgotten person, who has been tortured and made to suffer a price suddenly. That's how grace works. It qualifies the unqualified and its understanding makes me call God "the rewarder of the unworthy." It took God loving us first when we didn't even deserve it to birth grace. He sent his only son to die and prove his love for us. In addition, God gave us authority and a new identity just by believing in his love.

Faith, on the other hand, is our identification tag as Christians. We first had faith (believed) and then got saved by Jesus Christ. Over time, our faith continually grows and gets firm in our journey as Christians. It isn't an entirely smooth journey, but I can categorically say from experience that intentionality in reading and understanding God's word including prayers helps us trust God and in turn, build up our belief in Christ."

He added, "prayer is an intimate communication with God and not necessarily, an avenue to pile up a bunch of wants and requests. It is a time to worship and commune with the One you believe in and, should be done by Christians regularly." "Dad", Adam called, "are you, in summary, saying that Faith is the belief we have in Jesus and it is made stronger as we become intimate with God?" "Yes, son," Josh answered. "And Grace is a dispensation birthed by salvation?" "Yes, Adam, and to add to what you just said, Grace reveals to us that although we still fall due to the flesh, we aren't identified as sinners anymore but as sons of God. We are constantly learning through the Holy Spirit in us, and he is gradually changing us to be just like Christ.

The truth is the flesh would not want to give up on controlling your mind and will. Grace is a process, which is not immediate but you will see the change clearly, even as you walk with God. Apostle Paul clearly stated in the bible that if we are ignorant of salvation and think we can be made right with God by ourselves, or instantly, we simply imply that Jesus should not have come to the world to suffer and die for all our sins," Josh elaborately answered.

"My God!" Adam exclaimed. "Dad, you just stated a rare truth." "I am just a vessel used by God to speak to you and others, son. You should always thank the Holy Spirit for the privilege to know the truth", Josh revealed."Thank you Holy Spirit," Adam said softly, turning his head to the window beside the table. He observed how beautiful the sun was shining and thought of how kind God is to humans. "God is good! Dad. He first loved us and proceeded to save us through his son. Now we are complete in Christ and enjoy every benefit as his children," he said as tears dropped slowly from his eyes. "What did we do to deserve this, dad? What did we do?" he asked. Josh stood up to draw his son close to his chest and gave him a warm hug. "Nothing son, we did nothing," Josh answered as he wiped Adam's eyes. They both sat down next to each other to continue their discussion.

"We should leave for the park in twenty minutes boys," Anne stated with excitement from the kitchen. She already planned a family picnic for the weekend with their neighbors and was trying to round up cooking for a fun time. "Son, never forget that God made you perfect and he has known your end, even from the beginning. He knows the end will be very beautiful, if only you choose to submit to His will and not yours. As much as God loves us, he gave us the power to choose the paths we wish to follow, but I will always advise anyone who cares to listen to choose Christ. I must add that we humans should quit thinking highly of ourselves. Even if we are to prove our self-confidence, we should make sure we glorify and acknowledge Christ as the source of our confidence," Josh said. He further stated, "God told Jeremiah in Jeremiah 1:5 that before he formed him in his mother's womb, he has known Jeremiah and God's plan for his life prevailed in His life." I would like to stress this. "What dad?" Adam asked. "Being a Christian is a lifestyle and not a religion. A Christian is a person who surrendered to Christ to learn, unlearn, relearn and grow into perfection in Christ. It takes patience and an understanding process. It also takes us trusting God's plan and purpose. Trust brings complete glory to God Himself at the end and to you, as well," Josh answered.

CHAPTER 6

LOVE, THE GREATEST OF THEM ALL

*For now, there are faith, hope, and love. But
of these three, the greatest is love.*

1Corinthians13:13

"Love is patient, love is kind, love respects, and it doesn't keep anger. God is love. God loves the world so much that he gave his only son to suffer and die for us. Love brought eternal life in Christ, it can be found in John 3:16. God's love nullifies our earthly definition of love as feelings. God defined love as an "action." Sending Christ to die rather than just flattering confirms that his love for us is ever true and can be trusted," Josh said.

"Before Jesus Christ died, he commanded us to love the Lord our God with all of our heart, and by loving God, we are to obey only him and put Christ at the center of our life. We aren't left out as we were instructed by Jesus to love our neighbors and pray for our enemies. When we do this, we will not find ourselves doing anything to hurt those around us. Love doesn't make us weak, it gives us strength and makes us wise," Josh added. "But loving others isn't easy, dad," Adam muttered, "people tend to take us for granted." "Like I said, son," Josh answered, "learning to love doesn't make us weak, it gives us strength. You must not rely on your own efforts to love other people; you must rely on the help of the Holy Spirit. I will give you a tip son, whenever anyone hurts you, learn to stay calm and ask God's spirit to help you. Most times, I just tell myself "they aren't acting in their identity," and that helps to calm me down. I also try to wait for the right time to either discuss or just ask the Holy Spirit to continue to help me love a person. This is why we are different from the world; the spirit of God makes us different from others. Yes! We get angry, betrayed and tend to react excessively, but we do not do anything outside the Holy Spirit. We only carry out what the spirit asks of us if we seek him at our most trying times. You can only give love freely when you understand the love God has for you and this is only revealed by His Spirit as well."

"All these are deep revelations," Adam sighed. "Indeed, they are!" Josh smiled, nodding his head repeatedly. "You see son, true Christianity can be summarised this way: You hear the message of the good news and then believe Christ saved you. You, in turn, surrender your life without rethink, trusting him that he will walk with you on your way to transformation," Josh added. "The conversations we've had has been indeed insightful, dad! I love you," Adam said, and he hugged Josh tightly like he didn't want to let go. I'm glad I could speak so truthfully to you, son. I love you too," Josh said, hugging his son.

"Let us pray," Josh said, releasing Adam from the tight hug and holding his hands. As they prayed, Anne was fully dressed and ready to get the car keys when she sighted them praying together. She paused for a moment, placing both hands clapped together on her nose, and thanking God for her family. She waited till they were done with the prayer and immediately shouted excitedly, "okay boys! Let's go have some fun!!"

Anne still had a lot on her mind as she drove to the park. She was pregnant!

ACKNOWLEDGEMENT

I would love to first thank my parents for allowing me to be myself and who God has called me to be. Although It took lots of time for them to understand, I am grateful to God that they yielded and provided all I needed to grow. I also would love to thank GRACE OUTREACH GLOBAL CHURCH AKURE, NIGERIA. My pastors, Apostle and Lady Ola Aigbogun. I appreciate how you both take your time to encourage us to know God for ourselves. It has been and, it's still a learning and growing journey for me.

Lastly, I want to specifically thank Dr. Awelewa and his team for their support, contributions, and reviews, pastor Femi oguntade for the beautiful book cover, Fowowe Tomiwa for helping out as well, and my dearest Ayotomide oluwaseun for being a support system in the course of writing this book.

To you reading this, I deeply love and appreciate your support.

I pray I will also celebrate great things with you all, Amen.

ABOUT THE AUTHOR

Temiloluwa Asagunla O.

Temiloluwa Oladele Asagunla is a Christian creative writer and the founder of a female-based organization. Having described herself as a work in progress, she is passionate about young girls and the Christian community.

She is versatile and has interests in music, social work, and lots more, contributing the little she has to these sectors.

While currently focusing on helping to inspire people on their Journey out of Guilt and Fear, she also recently launched a project: "LET'S FIND YOU." With the hope of placing young girls on the path of becoming valuable.

She desires to push the truth of grace and Christian living as much as she can.